"Let's go fishing, George," said the man
with the yellow hat. They took their
fishing poles and drove to the country.

"This looks like a good place,"
said the man.

Curious George®
GOES FISHING

Colin

Adapted from the Curious George film series
edited by Margret Rey and Alan J. Shalleck

1 9 8 7
Houghton Mifflin Company, Boston

Library of Congress Cataloging-in-Publication Data

Curious George goes fishing.

"Adapted from the Curious George film series."
Summary: Curious George's interest in helping a
fisherman catch more fish ends in disaster, but he
is able to redeem himself later.
[1. Monkeys—Fiction.   2. Fishing—Fiction]
I. Rey, Margret.   II. Shalleck, Alan J.   III. Curious
George goes fishing (Motion picture)
PZ7.C92137   1987   [E]   87-9282
ISBN 0-395-45351-8

"I'll look for a shallow spot. You wait here, George,
and don't get into trouble."

While George waited,
he decided to swing through the trees.

From one tree, George saw a family having a picnic.
The mother and two little girls
were preparing lunch. The father was fishing.

Sometimes he caught a fish.
Sometimes he didn't.

When his basket was full of fish,
the man took it back to his family.

George was curious.
Could he fish, too?

He climbed down from the tree
and picked up the pole.

But when George tried to throw out the line,

the hook caught on the family's frying pan
full of fish.

George pulled as hard as he could.
He pulled and he pulled and he

pulled the whole pan off the fire.

It flipped high into the air.
The family's lunch went flying.

"Oh, no," the mother cried,
"there goes our lunch!"

George was scared.

He hid in the trees.

Now, when the father tried to catch more fish,
his luck was bad.

Finally, he gave up, and the family
went to see if they had
any other food in their car.

Now George could come down.

He picked up some pebbles and threw them
into the water to pass the time.

Just then a fish leaped up.
Then another.
Then two more.

So this is where the fish are!
Now George knew what to do.

Meanwhile, the family came back.
They had not found any food.
"I guess I'll try to fish again," said the father.

But when he turned back to the brook,
the fishing poles were gone!
Then the family saw something else.

"Look!" shouted one of the little girls.

George was fishing with all four fishing poles.

"He's got a bite!" the little girl cried.
"Two bites!" said her sister.
"Three!" said the father.

George tugged and tugged.
And he caught four fat shiny fish!

George and the man with the yellow hat
were invited to lunch. It was delicious.
Especially for George, the fisherman.